Anonymous

Address to the Laity of the Diocese of Quebec from the Church of England

SALZWASSER
VERLAG

Anonymous

Address to the Laity of the Diocese of Quebec from the Church of England

Reprint of the original, first published in 1859.

1st Edition 2022 | ISBN: 978-3-37512-164-8

Verlag (Publisher): Salzwasser Verlag GmbH, Zeilweg 44, 60439 Frankfurt, Deutschland
Vertretungsberechtigt (Authorized to represent): E. Roepke, Zeilweg 44, 60439 Frankfurt, Deutschland
Druck (Print): Books on Demand GmbH, In de Tarpen 42, 22848 Norderstedt, Deutschland

ADDRESS

TO THE

LAITY OF THE DIOCESE

OF QUEBEC,

FROM THE

CHURCH OF ENGLAND

Lay Association.

SECOND EDITION.

WITH AN APPENDIX,

CONTAINING A PROPOSED

CONSTITUTION FOR THE SYNOD;

ALSO THE

ACTS OF PARLIAMENT

WHICH AUTHORIZE THE ASSEMBLING THEREOF;

AND OTHER NEW MATTER.

Quebec:

MIDDLETON & DAWSON, PRINTERS, SHAW'S BUILDINGS.

1859.

Preface to the Second Edition.

Since the publication of the first edition of the following Address, several notices, both *pro* and *con*, of the subjects on which it treats, have emanated from unknown sources. The Lay Association, however, when issuing a second edition to meet the increasing demand, might be excused the task of alluding, at any length, to the productions of anonymous objectors, even if these had disturbed the position of the Association, and if the courtesy and temper of the most elaborate of them, had been developed in more polished and becoming phraseology. As it is, they are content to reflect that such sentiments and epithets as have been unjustly pointed at the members of the Association, seldom indicate a good cause, and do not reflect much credit on a weak one.

With reference to the five points, of varying importance, dwelt upon in their Address, it is satisfactory to the Association to find that no particular objection is made to their views relative to the 1st, 3rd, and 4th ; and although the 2nd and 5th have been criticized more at large, they see no reason to modify the sentiments which they have expressed. With respect to the former, (viz., the qualifications of lay delegates,) the theory that the partaking of the eucharist includes all necessary qualifications, is so clearly contradicted by practical experience, that the Association cannot but adhere to the opinion that the people are the best judges of the fitness of their representatives, and should not be restricted, further than they now are by law, in the choice of their delegates. With respect to the latter, (viz., the claimed Episcopal *Veto*,)* it may be observed that a voluntary transition from the autocratic to a constitutional form of government, necessarily involves fundamental but beneficial changes, whether taking place in the State or in the Church, and that it may not be expected, in such a case, to blend two uncongenial forms, by retaining in the new one, incompatible characteristics of the old. The constitutional principle, once adopted, should be consistently carried out. It seems, indeed, to be admitted, as regards the Synod, that " everything" (including, therefore, the *Veto*) " will depend upon the nature and provisions of the Constitution, which it will be the first duty of the Synod to construct." This concession, moreover, is implied in the pains which have been taken to argue upon this matter of the *Veto*, as also upon the others relative to lay qualifications, &c. Where everything, then, is confessedly to derive its synodical existence from the tenor of the

---

* The latest modification of the *Veto* which has been proposed is, that an appeal should lie from it to a Provincial Synod, where a separate house of Bishops would sustain the principle of Episcopal Government. But,

1st.—This is at once to confess what is alleged, viz : that the *Veto* absolute ought not to be entrusted to one man.·

2nd.—No Provincial Synod is in existence ; there may never be one ; and it will at least be soon enough when there is, for the Synod to consider this proposition.

3rd.—Being confessedly unsafe to grant a *Veto* without appeal, it would further be improper, until it shall have been ascertained that a Provincial Synod, when constituted, would accept an Appellate Jurisdiction, and upon what questions.

4th.—It will, on all accounts, be prudent to try the Synodical experiment first without the *Veto*, since this may at any time be granted, if found desirable ; but if once granted, it cannot be revoked.

Constitution that may be adopted, there can be no ante-
cedent rights, nor inherent privileges. The Association
are, therefore, confirmed in their principle that everything
regarding the Synod will depend upon the Constitution ;
and again, that whatever the Constitution may confer, the
Constitution may withhold ; especially when it is considered that the law does not prescribe any provisions of a
Constitution, nor recognize beforehand any prerogatives
of orders, nor sanction any particular model for the Synod, but leaves " the Bishop, Clergy, and Laity," (who
are specified merely as comprised in the more comprehen-
sive and generic designation of, " Members of the United
Church of England and Ireland)" free, " in such manner
and by such proceedings as they shall adopt, to frame
constitutions and make regulations, &c." for the government of the Church. Nor will the Association be deter-
red by any misrepresentations of their motives and aims
from loyally desiring to see the foundations of the Church
in this Diocese laid in the liberty of the Laity, the independence of the Clergy, and the constitutional prerogatives of the Bishop.

ADDRESS.

The Church of England Lay Association, recently formed in the City of Quebec, take an early opportunity of inviting the attention of their lay brethren throughout the Diocese, to the nature and objects of the Association, and of placing before them a few considerations connected with the important rights and duties about to devolve upon the Church in the present new aspect of ecclesiastical affairs.

The circumstances which naturally gave rise to the Association, have, together with its general character and designs, been sufficiently explained in a Report* of a Committee appointed on the 26th July last, at a public meeting of the members of the Church ; and which was adopted at a similar meeting held at the Court-House, on the 2nd September following, when also the Association was formed. Referring, therefore, to that document for a narrative of past transactions, it is only proposed, on the present occasion, to glance at a few of the more important considerations which necessarily come under review in connection with the powers of synodical action and self-government, now by law conferred upon the Church. In doing this, however, the Lay Association desire to be

---

* This document which contained a sketch of transactions previous to the formation of the Association, is substituted in this issue by the *Acts of Parliament* which authorize Synodical action in the Church ; the proximity of the Easter elections rendering it desirable that these should be generally circulated for the information and guidance of the constituencies.

distinctly understood as presuming neither to dictate nor to prescribe to the Laity at large the opinions they should hold, or the line of conduct they should pursue, in the exercise of their newly acquired privileges. Neither do they so much pretend to impart instruction, where, comparatively speaking, all are novices ; as, by conference, either in writing, or verbally, or both, to elicit the real sentiments of the people, in order that these may be ultimately concentrated in the legislature of the Church.

The general interests of the Laity are identical in all parts of the Diocese alike : neither those of the city, nor those of the towns, nor those of the rural districts, have any inducement to over-reach each other ; nor can anything which ministers to the welfare of the Laity *en masse*, be otherwise than conducive to the general welfare of the Church. The Association is, accordingly, open to all her adult members without distinction ; and all are invited to enrol their names amongst its members, upon a perfect footing of equality, wherever they may happen to reside. Its objects are to ascertain and make public the views of the Laity upon the important subject-matters about to be confided to the Synod ; to secure, thus, for the Church, the proper influence of the known opinions and wants of the masses of her members ; and for their delegates, ability to discharge their important functions with satisfaction to themselves, and advantage to the Church at large. The methods by which it is proposed to accomplish these ends, are comprised in a simple interchange of sentiment and experience upon questions falling within the range of synodical legislation. And while humbly yet freely expressing their own views, as occasion may require, upon such questions, the Association invite the fullest communication of the views of others, in order that a genuine public opinion upon matters affecting the dearest privileges of the present and succeeding generations, may be created in the Diocese, so that when the time shall arrive for the election of the delegates, the several congregations may the more intelligently exercise their elective franchise, instruct their representatives accordingly, and thus render the Constitution and proceedings of the Synod, as regards its lay element, a true reflection of the opinions and wishes of the great body of the Church.

It is presumed to be generally known that, under the authority of recent statutes, (19 & 20 Vic., cap. 121, and 22 Vic., cap. 139,*) the Bishop, Clergy and Laity may meet, (the latter by representation,) and frame constitutions and regulations for the discipline, government, and management of the property and affairs of their respective Dioceses. This convention in each Diocese will be a *Diocesan Synod.* They may also, by such representatives as shall be determined in the several Dioceses, meet in *General Assembly*, and frame a Constitution for the general management and government of the Church in the entire Province. The Diocesan Synod and the General Assembly thus contemplated, bear evident analogy to the admirably constituted and successful Diocesan and General Conventions of the Protestant Episcopal Church in the United States. It is, however, of matters pertaining to the Diocesan Synod exclusively, that the Association are at present called upon to treat. The earliest attention of that body, when assembled in its first session at the summons of the Lord Bishop, must be given to the construction of a Constitution which may regulate its own subsequent composition and proceedings, and make other provisions contemplated by the law. Possibly the articles of such an instrument need not be very numerous, at least until additions and amendments, in the form of canons or otherwise, shall have been suggested by

---

* See Appendix A.

future experience of the requirements of the Church. A Constitution, however, of some kind, will be indispensable *in limine*, to give organized form to a legislative assembly invested by law with very extensive powers and authority ; and although it might be deemed presumptuous and premature, were the Association to throw their ideas into a draft of a Constitution, and to publish it for the information of the public ; yet, as a document of that description, which was framed by a Committee previous to the date of their formation, has been laid upon their table, and generally commends itself to their approval, they append it to this Address,* to serve at least as a basis for the free conference upon the subject to which they respectfully invite their lay brethren throughout the Diocese. But in the meantime, their attention has been directed particularly to certain points of such prominent importance in reference to the matter of a Constitution, that they venture at once to allude to these somewhat in detail. And

1stly.—With reference to the boundaries of the several constituencies, and the number of delegates from each, it is perhaps of less consequence than is commonly supposed, whether every separate congregation, however small, in each mission or pastoral charge, should form a separate constituency, and send its delegates to Synod ; or whether each entire pastoral charge should form but one constituency. The latter, rather than the former, plan accords with prevailing precedent, and with equity, and is the one suggested in the draft of a constitution hereunto appended. But whether either of these, or a different one based upon population, be adopted by the Synod, the Association recommend that each constituency be allowed to elect three delegates, as at present permitted to do by

* See Appendix B.

law. The advantages to a delegate, of having an associate interested in the same locality to confer with, are considerable ; while the election of three will diminish the chances of there being any one constituency entirely unrepresented.

2ndly.—As regards the qualifications of the delegates, the Association are clearly of opinion that the electors in each constituency are the best judges of the fitness of their representatives, and that to restrict their liberty in the choice of their delegates, would be a needless and dangerous interference with the elective franchise of the people. The idea has, nevertheless, more than once been seriously proposed, to limit eligibility to the office of a delegate to communicants ; and as it may be proposed again, it may not be unnecessary to expend a few words upon the subject. The motive for the proposal may be presumed to be the good one of securing for the Synod the presence of well-qualified representatives. Apart, however, from the consideration that the Laity are the safest guardians of their own interests, and the best judges of the suitableness of candidates for their votes, there is the further one that the partaking of the sacred ordinance in question does not necessarily imply the possession of superior qualifications. It were doubtless desirable that every member of the Church appreciated all her articles, practised all her precepts, and conformed to all her ordinances ; and *that* upon the ground of their being based upon the supreme authority of the Word of God. It is also especially desirable that the qualifications of intelligence, honesty, and personal piety, should be attributes of every member of the Synod, clerical as well as lay. But it is difficult to discover why, out of the whole catalogue of the doctrines, moral requirements, sacramental and ceremonial observances of the Church, one in particular should be selected as the stepping-stone to synodical honors, and the sole standard of personal suitableness for the important trust of a lay delegate ; or, why all the other characteristics of consistent churchmanship, and even all the delinquencies of the inconsistent professor, should be overlooked, and the mere participation of the eucharist be made the sole test of eligibility for the approval and confidence of the constituencies. It should be remembered that conscientious scruples of various kinds are amongst the influences which deter some consistent members of the Church from approaching the Sacramental table. May not this very tenderness of conscience which actuates them, itself supply the strongest possible security, if accepting the functions of a delegate, that they will faithfully and conscientiously discharge them ? It is further to be considered that the adoption of the sacramental qualification for all lay delegates would, in this country, in some cases, so circumscribe the choice of the people, as virtually to destroy it, if, indeed, it might not in others compel them, in order to be represented at all, to elect parties the least able to represent, or who would actually misrepresent them. The question must be regarded as belonging exclusively to the Laity ; and, if handled as a general one of peremptory discipline, especially if so mooted in order to exalt the sacramental power of the Clergy, may open up other questions of deviation from the usages of the Church, and awaken undesirable discussions. If to communicate once a year be exacted as a qualification, why not once a month ? why not also attendance in the Church at daily prayer, and on all the " saints' days," with other rubrical requirements, not more arbitrary, nor less questionable, as tests of genuine Christianity ? True, it may be urged that, in some secular elections, material guarantees are demanded for the loyalty of the elected ; and that attendance at the Lord's table implies a guarantee for the piety which includes all other qualifications.

Where religious interests, however, are concerned,
every man's stake in the welfare of the Church
of which he is a member, is already, presumably,
a sufficient warranty of his integrity ; but even if
this were otherwise, do not the walk and conversation,
both public and private, of some regular communicants,
furnish lamentable proof, that, if unable to govern
themselves according to the principles of the Church, they
cannot be pre-eminently qualified to govern her ? The
wide and delicate question of personal Church-discipline,
may, appropriately, at a future day, engage attention, if it
do not also excite some feeling, in the Synod ; but until
dealt with as a whole, it would be inconvenient and
unjust to legislate partially upon the subject. Can it be
presumed to comport with peculiar fitness for a legislator
of the Church, to give but little or none of his goods to
feed the poor,—to take God's name in vain,—to desecrate
the Sabbath by secular amusements or pursuits,—to in-
dulge in intemperate habits,—to slander or defraud his
neighbour,—to be early on the turf, and late at the gaming
table ; provided only that the Table of the Lord be ap-
proached once a year, to preserve his synodical ortho-
doxy ? Or, can the interests of religion imperatively require the eligibility of such an one to Synod, merely because
he is a communicant, and the exclusion of the moral and
conscientious churchman, merely because he is not ? If it be
a duty to deplore the above inconsistencies, can it be, at
the same time, a duty to ignore them, and to magnify the
simple outward observance of a most solemn ordinance
into an atoning service which shall cover a multitude of
such delinquencies (itself, perhaps, the greatest of all)
and invest, it may be, some mere ambitious formalist with
an exclusive title to the suffrages, without the confidence,
of the electors ? No such condition as that of the sacramental test is sought to be imposed on those clergymen.
who, being without cure of souls, are not required by the

rubric to partake of the ordinance in question, but who will, nevertheless, take their seats in the Synod : neither need it be imposed upon the Laity.* The odious and demoralizing provisions of the Test and Corporation Act, have long been erased from the statute-book of the mother-country. The Association have no desire to see them revived in the Constitution of a Colonial Church. The law has qualified as electors " all laymen of the full age of twenty-one years, who shall declare themselves, in writing, to be members of the United Church of England and Ireland, and to belong to no other religious denomination." The Association conceive that all such electors should continue to be, as they now are, eligible to be members of the Synod.

3rdly.—With respect to the assembling and proroguing of the Synod—a subject which, although involving to a large extent the liberty and independence of the Synod, may not require much argument—the Association are of

---

* A proposition to that effect having been made and negatived in the Diocese of Pennsylvania, in 1847, " the Bishop, previous to giving his vote, which was in the negative, gave some reasons for his course ; that he greatly desired the accomplishment of the object, but thought that the end was likely to be attained by means less stringent ; that the sudden and peremptory exclusion of non-communicants would leave some parishes without any representation—would cast out several exemplary members—and would impair the influence of pastors over many non-communicants who were kept from the table rather by pious scruples than indifference."

In the Convention of the Diocese of New York, in 1849, " the subject was largely and thoroughly discussed, and the proposed amendment" (viz : requiring delegates to be communicants,) " was lost by a non-concurrence of orders."

The subject being revived in the same Diocese, in 1858, it was indefinitely postponed, on the recommendation of the Bishop, who said " For several years my attention has been turned to it at different times, and the more I have considered it in the light of all the facts, the less I have felt inclined to favor it."

B

opinion that a session of that body should be held at a fixed time and place in every year, and that its proceedings should be liable to adjournment, only upon its own rule or resolution. The Act of Parliament empowers the Bishop to summon the first meeting; but the Synod, once assembled, will become the supreme authority in the Church in all matters affecting itself; and the Association humbly suggest that it will be the duty of the delegates to consent to no provision in the Constitution, tending to deprive the Synod of the right to hold its future meetings for business, at a period to be defined in that document; and, to adjourn them at its own discretion. It is gratifying to the Association to observe that the principle of this recommendation corresponds with the view of their own Diocesan; who, in 1851, " considered it desirable that the Bishop, Clergy, and Laity in each Diocese should meet together in Synod, at such times and in such manner as may be agreed."* If otherwise, the power to convoke might become so latent as virtually to make void the Synod, by never calling it together at all; and the power to prorogue be so wielded as to destroy all freedom of debate; since it would be competent to the authority possessing it to stop all proceedings in the middle of an unwelcome discussion; or, by threatening this, to silence any member, clerical or lay, at a pointed turn of an unpalatable speech, or indeed if he presumed to speak at all. If lodged with the Bishop, the power here reviewed would be an Episcopal *Veto* in its most objectionable form.

4thly.—The excellent provision for a "vote by orders," in an assembly composed of mixed classes, next requires some notice from the Association. It is commended in a recent public document as " a wholesome usage; conservative of the rights of the Clergy and Laity alike; obtaining universally in the Diocesan and General Conventions of the sister-Church in the United States; and

* See "Minutes of a Conference of the Bishops, &c."

transcribed from her excellent models into recent organizations of the Colonial Church. It is, however, utterly without precedent in the mother-Church of England and Ireland ; is known, wherever it exists, not as an inherent or abstract right, but only as a constitutional privilege ; and cannot, therefore, vest in the clerical or lay elements of a Synod, any more than can a *Veto*, absolute or qualified, vest in the Bishop, until authorized by a Constitution lawfully adopted by the Church." The Association do not anticipate any material difference of opinion respecting the insertion in the Constitution of the necessary provision for the safeguard of the " vote by orders." Nevertheless, it may supply not wholly superfluous information to some readers of this Address, if the Association offer a few remarks regarding that convenient and equitable method of combining the clerical and lay talent of the Church, for purposes of deliberation, in a single assembly, and yet of obtaining, when desired, the separate judgment of each, without detriment to the interests of either. It is believed to be an American invention, and loses none of its intrinsic value from being found everywhere in the tried machinery of that well organized Episcopal Church already referred to, to which the Colonial Church must look for other patterns of Constitutional Church-government, and of a flourishing Episcopacy. The "orders" of the above technical expression are not the three orders of the ministry—Bishop, Priests, and Deacons—as if each of these, besides the Laity, making in all four elements, might exercise, on demand, a separate voice ; but they are merely the two classes of the Clergy and Laity which compose the Convention. And the meaning of the "vote by orders" is, that, while in ordinary cases these two classes deliberate and vote together without distinction, they may, when desired, on special occasions, particularly when interests peculiar to either are at stake, vote separately, or " by orders ;" and when that is done, no measure is held to be adopted unless obtaining a majority of both orders—i. e., a majority of the Clergy, voting apart ; and a majority of the Laity, voting apart ; or a "concurrent majority," as it is termed. Thus, neither order can override or overbear the other, and the "vote by orders" becomes a security for the rights and interests of both.

5thly.—The last topic upon which the Association deem it necessary here to speak, is the so-called "Episcopal *Veto*." It cannot be pretended or expected, within the compass of a single section of an Address, that a subject which has been dealt with so fully as this has been, both verbally and through the medium of the press, should receive from the Association more than a passing notice of some of its leading features. It is claimed, as an essential attribute of the Episcopate, that the Bishop should possess the power of an absolute negative upon any measure of the Synod, carried by whatever separate majorities of both its orders. That any such autocratic authority is essential to the Episcopate, is sufficiently refuted by the notorious fact that there are upwards of thirty organized Dioceses of the Protestant Episcopal Church in the United States, in which the Bishops are clothed with no such prerogative. To hold, therefore, that the *Veto* is essential to the Episcopate, is at once to unconsecrate upwards of thirty prelates of a Church which has enlarged her borders, and multiplied her Sees, during the last seventy-five years, without conferring any such power upon her Bishops.— The small and unprogressive *Diocese of Vermont is the

---

* The justness of the sentiment suggested here, having been questioned, the following statistics are supplied for the reader's information :—

DIOCESES.	No. of Clergy.		DIOCESES.	No. of Clergy.	
	1839.	1857.		1839.	1857.
Vermont	22	23	New York	171	309
Maine	5	17	Western New York	75	118
New Hampshire	7	13	New Jersey	39	85
Massachusetts	50	77	Pennsylvania	91	165
Rhode Island	18	32	Delaware	10	20
Connecticut	79	118	Maryland	71	144

solitary exception to the prevailing rule. No other pre-cedent for it has been produced, except that it has been very recently yielded in some newly-formed Colonial Synods with untried Constitutions. The Association frank-ly avow their preference for the well-tried system which has worked so efficiently in the sister-Church of the adjoining States. Nor can they perceive the wisdom or safety of substituting, in this respect, for the happy example which that Church presents, needless experiments and untried inventions in ecclesiastical legislation, at variance with the constitutional principles, prevailing precedents, and successful experience, during three quarters of a century, of that most perfectly organized Protestant Episcopal Church in the world.

It is, indeed, impossible for the Association to compre-hend the consistency of desiring a Synod at all, and at the same time of investing its presiding officer with the power of nullifying its proceedings; and particularly under the now recognized principle of an elective Episcopate. In, perhaps, the most important act of the Synod—the elec-tion of a Bishop—there can, obviously, be no *Veto*. Yet, by what reasoning can it be shewn that the Synod, which, proceeding to the choice of a Bishop, and therefore without a Bishop presiding in it, is competent to sit in

DIOCESES.	No. of Clergy. 1839.	1857.	DIOCESES.	No of Clergy. 1839.	1857.
Virginia	75	118	Michigan	20	41
North Carolina	22	45	Louisiana	2	34
South Carolina	46	66	Indiana	8	26
Georgia	8	22	Missouri	6	23
Ohio	54	83	Illinois	13	45
Mississippi	6	30	Wisconsin	4	46
Kentucky	20	30			
Tennessee	19	17		949	1776
Alabama	8	20			

NEWER DIOCESES.		NEWER DIOCESES.	
D. of Florida	7	Indian Territory	3
D. of Iowa	20	D of California	12
D. of Arkansas	4	Oregon and Washington Territory	7
D. of Texas	16		86
North West Mission	17		

judgment upon a matter of the weightiest import, must forfeit, the moment the new Bishop is elected, its competency to legislate in the smallest matters, and remain thus paralyzed, until his death resuscitate its dormant competency to perform anew the waking act of a fresh election, and then to fall again into a trance? Would not this be virtually to limit the functions of the Synod to the election of Bishops?

But the Act of Parliament (19 & 20 Vic., cap. 121,) empowers the Synod in every Diocese to " make regulations for enforcing discipline in the Church, for the appointment, deposition, deprivation, or removal, of any person bearing office therein, of whatever order or degree." Is it not perfectly legitimate to imagine, for a moment, the case of the trial of a Bishop, or the proposal of a Canon for establishing a Court for that purpose, and for regulating its proceedings? and is it not perfectly absurd to suppose that the Synod would have liberty in the premises, if the Bishop had been previously endowed with an absolute *Veto* upon all its enactments? Nay, the unanimous votes of the Clergy and Laity, in Synod assembled, would be powerless for the " exclusion from the meetings or proceedings of the Synod," (which the said Act also authorizes,) of the humblest of its members, clerical or lay, whatever might be the proved charges against him, if he but happen to enjoy a sufficient amount of Episcopal favor and support, to secure for him a *Veto* upon the resolution for his expulsion. The Synod would thus be deprived of the right—inherent in all independent deliberative bodies—of purging its own floor, and protecting its own privileges. Again, if the Synod be qualified to choose a Bishop for the Diocese, by what rule of propriety or of common sense, may he, on the day of his election, turn round on his electors, and, by a *Veto* upon all their measures, except that of his own elevation, declare them disqualified to judge of all other requirements of the Church? If the Bishop for the time being, concentrated in his one mind all the wisdom and experience of the Church; and in his sympathies all her wants; and were gifted with the attribute of infallibility; reason might that he should be entrusted with uncontrolled authority. But the best of men are fallible; and the wisest of fallible men are too distrustful of their own exercise of unrestricted power to covet it; lest their own opinions and acts should be swayed by private predilections, rather than the public good. What prerogative, then, can be fraught with greater danger to the Bishop himself, as well as to the Church, than that which is contended for as "essential to the Episcopate?" The five Bishops themselves, indeed, (viz., of Quebec, Toronto, Newfoundland, Fredericton, and Montreal,) appear to have been conscious of this when (in their "Minutes of a Conference of the Bishops, holden at Quebec from September 24th to October 1st, 1851,") they adduce it as the one ground of their desire for a Synod, that they "experience great difficulty in acting in accordance with their Episcopal Commission and Prerogatives, and their decisions are liable to misconstruction, as if emanating from their individual will, and not from the general body of the Church." It would be difficult to describe or to deprecate the Episcopal *Veto* of a synodical enactment, in more appropriate or stronger terms, than as a "decision emanating from the individual will of the Bishop," despite the expressed wishes of "the general body of the Church." It is with unmingled satisfaction, therefore, that the Association thus read the recorded opinion of these high authorities, including their own Diocesan, as harmonizing, in this particular, so completely with their own. *

---

* A Church of England author, of grave character and great experience, says : " An absolute *Veto* is neither safe, nor belongs to the essence of an Episcopal Church-system. Surely it is pos-

The Association scarcely deem it necessary to pursue at any length the fallacious and exploded argument attempted to be drawn from a supposed analogy between the three estates of the realm, and the three (which however, strictly speaking, are either four—Bishop, Priests, Deacons, and Laity, or only two—Clergy and Laity,) of the Church ; and then between the prerogative of the Queen and the *Veto* of the President on the one hand, and the claimed *Veto* of a Bishop on the other. But there is no analogy. The prerogative of the Crown of England is now on all hands conceded to be, to all practical intents and purposes, a constitutional, not an arbitrary, prerogative, to be used by and with the consent of the Ministry, her constitutional advisers, who are responsible to the

---

sible to be a very good Episcopalian, without admitting that a Bishop necessarily knows better than any conceivable majority of a united body of clergy and lay delegates." " If a majority of the clergy, and a majority of the laity, voting separately, be obtained in favor of a measure, it ought not to be finally negatived by any one individual." " The prevailing repugnance to the concession of the *Veto* has been expressed mainly with reference to the *one-man-power* ; no one individual ought to be thus entrusted with the authority of negativing the united decision of his fellows." " Our sister-church in the United States has got along these sixty years, and has prospered, without this ' essential feature' of an Episcopal Church." And another—"As the head of the clergy, the Bishop, sitting with them, will always exercise as much influence as one man ought to have in a deliberative body, particularly amongst a dependent missionary-clergy. To give him more than that proper weight which office, talents, and piety, will always secure, by allowing him to step aside from the body in which he had been conducting a debate, in order to *veto* an adopted measure upon which he had been deliberating, would not only destroy the independence of the Church, but in the end endanger the Episcopate itself." " The *Veto* is a power which would clothe its possessor with an accumulation of prerogatives not less foreign as a whole to a Scriptural Episcopate, than would this one in particular be dangerous to the independence of the Church."

people. And the *Veto* of the President of the United States, who is himself directly responsible to the public voice, is subject to wholesome checks, both legislative and personal. If, pending his brief term of office, the *Veto* any Bill, he must return it with his reasons ; and if it be re-affirmed by a two-thirds vote of the Legislature, his *Veto* is annulled, and the measure, *ipso facto*, becomes law. But further, he is himself subject at the hustings to the people's quadrennial *Veto* upon him. If the analogy were made complete by surrounding the Episcopal chair with a body of constitutional advisers, amenable to the Synod ; or by subjecting both the claimed *Veto* of its occupant to the overbearing voice of the Synod, and also its occupant himself periodically to a synodical re-election, the *Veto* of the Bishop would become, in such a case, not an arbitrary power, but a constitutional privilege, for which his "Ministry" in the one case, and both his decision and himself in the other, would be, at recurring periods, responsible to the Church. The Association, however, question whether either of these arrangements would accord with the genius of Episcopacy ; and still more whether a quadrennial election of a Bishop would be less dangerous to the peace of the Church, than a *Veto* absolute would be to her liberty. But the pretended analogy still further fails when it is remembered that neither of the above secular functionaries sits or deliberates in the Senate of either country. " In no case," observes an English writer, " can it be safe or constitutitional to centre the double functions of the legislative and executive in one and the same hands. Neither the Sovereign nor the President has a seat or a vote in Parliament, and even their *Veto* is guarded by constitutional restraints which make it virtually subject to the voice of the nation, as the functions of all her members, clerical and lay, ought to be subject to the authority of the Church. The *Veto* would place one of them above it."

It only remains, in connection with this subject, to notice the deadening influence which the known possession of a *Veto* by the Bishop must needs exert upon the vitality of the Synod in which he presides.   The object of the Synod is to obtain a full and free expression of the wants and wishes of the Church ; and, as far as practicable, to provide for them.   Towards the accomplishment of these ends, she invites her members to lay all their treasures of wisdom and knowledge, of intellect and influence, of zeal and experience, at her feet.   Everything, therefore, tending to restrain them in the conception, advocacy, and completion, of wholesome measures for her welfare, would be a barrier to the attainment of the object of the Synod. The clerical element in that body, being an assemblage of several individuals, is deliberative in character—differing, discussing, voting, amongst themselves ; and a majority preponderates : so also is the Lay element.   Under such circumstances, truth is elicited in the freedom of debate, and the issue is the result of fair deliberation.   But, let a chilling feeling brood over the Synod, that a distinct party is present, who is not a deliberative element, cannot argue with himself, nor d'ride upon a question within himself, but whose own "individual will" can outweigh all the united logic and judgment of the Synod ; and how paralysing to every manly and independent thought, valuable design, and forcible argument—how destructive of the end and purpose of a conference—must be the incubus of such a feeling !   How useless to propose, or to reason, or for the Synod to waste its time by entertaining a motion or a suggestion until, first, the leaning and wishes of the Bishop be disclosed !   The first enquiry with every member, with respect to any project for the Church's good, will be— not, is it in itself, and in its season, a desirable one ? but, what are the Bishop's projects, the Bishop's wishes, the Bishop's interests, or predilections, or even prejudices !

And thus, the energy and independence of the Synod withered, and its design defeated, it will become little else than an office of record for enregistering the acts of the Bishop, performed under the misnomer of Synodical legislation. " It would be quite as well," remarks a writer already quoted, " to do without the semblance of legislation, as to be called upon to legislate within the limits which the existence of the *Veto* would assign to the Church's representatives." And an American writer says :—" A *Veto*, vested in a sitting and acting member of the legislative body, destroys legislative freedom altogether. If the President has the right of thus annulling the legislative will, the attempt to legislate in his presence is a farce, and free discussion worse than useless. His vote in the negative on any proposition would, of course, destroy it, even on a preliminary question ; for there would be a manifest impropriety in any further proceedings, which would be both disrespectful to him, and derogatory to the dignity of the house. But the chief reason why, in our political institutions, the *Veto* is never connected with legislative membership, applies with peculiar force to the Church. When so associated, it absorbs in its possessor absolute power. ' This, I will not pass in this shape,'* not only prevents the introduction of an unwelcome subject, but exacts its modification so as to connect with the *Veto*-power the power of initiation." The Bishop examines, ordains, and licenses all clergymen, who, if ever leaving the Diocese, require his letters dimissory or commendatory: in this Diocese, in the present instance, as Rector of Quebec (an office held unavoidably together with the Episco-

---

* " If I recollect right," (states an English author,) " the Bishop of Vermont says, it does not happen that he has to exercise the *Veto* which the Constitution gives him ; for when Clergy and Laity discuss a matter which the Bishop is decidedly opposed to, he just gets up and says so ; then they desist, and the matter drops ! This is precisely what I suppose the Emperor of Russia does in his Council of Ministers or Generals !"

pal)—besides the clerical patronage of the Cathedral or Parish-Church—he is the patron of three or four Chapelries ; 'he is Visitor of a College which will probably send three or four more clergymen to Synod ; and as Agent of the " Society for the Propagation of the Gospel in Foreign Parts," as well as of the " Church Society," he is the patron and paymaster of country Missionaries, locates and removes them. No calculation is here made of the number of clerical votes which he may thus directly and indirectly command ; nor of the lay votes which, through the clergy, he may command also.* It cannot be denied that an immense and varied, if not alarming amount of official, moral, and material influence clusters thus already around the Episcopal chair. Surely it cannot be " essential to the Episcopate," nor necessary nor safe for the Church, that this concentration of power— which is unknown to the Hierarchy of the United Church of England and Ireland ; is also without precedent in the United States ; and which, it is believed, finds no parallel even in the Church of Rome—should be increased and consummated by adding to it, besides a presiding influence in the Synod, a *Veto* upon all its transactions.† If under

---

* It was publicly boasted by a Clergyman, on a late occasion, that he had a thousand people in his mission, who would vote exactly as he desired them !

† The subject here in hand is illustrated by recent information from the Diocese of Nova Scotia, where—in the Synod which assembled in October last—" Notice was given of a motion to abolish the Bishop's *Veto* over the proceedings of the Synod, and to compel him to preside with his council in a separate room, that the deliberations of the Synod might be more free and unbiassed." —(*Church Witness.*) The fact is pregnant with instruction relative to the possession of undue and anomalous powers, and to the working of untried Constitutions. The experiment of the *Veto* is already furnishing matter for discontent and agitation in the Church, which are not likely to be diminished by the reflection that the Bishop may *Veto* any attempt of the Synod to deprive him of the *Veto* with which the Constitution has endowed him.

such circumstances, and notwithstanding all the *prestige* of his office, and the weight of his patronage, any measure ever receive a majority of the clerical and lay votes, contrary to the wishes of the Bishop, the simple fact would certainly indicate a case in which his own "individual will" ought not to outweigh and nullify the decision of such a concurrent majority. The Association, however, do not overlook the consideration that there are imperfections in every human organization, and that there will be disadvantages as well as advantages attendant upon a union of the Clergy and Laity in one house. The latter are those of better personal acquaintance, and amicable interchange of thought : the former those, occasionally, of warm debate, and precipitate decisions. With the view of meeting the contingency of oversights and hasty legislation, the draft of a Constitution hereunto annexed* proposes to endow the Episcopate with a reserving power, (i. e. a power to reserve a measure, even though it should have been passed by both orders, for reconsideration at the next meeting of the Synod,) which promises adequate provision for every inconvenience. The Association respectfully recommend it, accordingly, to the favorable consideration of the Church generally.†

Having thus adverted, as originally proposed, to a few of the more important subject-matters about to be confided

---

* See Appendix A.

† The Lord Bishop of Huron, at the recent meeting of the Synod of that Diocese. stated, in reference to the *Veto*, that " he considered that it imposed a very heavy responsibility on him to be possessed of such power as proposed, and he thought that after two years' deliberation he would be acting against every right were he not to accede to the repeated request of the majority of the Synod."—*Echo*, 30th Sept., 1858. This view exactly reduces the *Veto* to the above " power to reserve for re-consideration,"— the only difference being that the Association prefer its being embodied in an Article of the Constitution.

C

tho present juncture of the affairs of the Church, the Association, in conclusion, earnestly hope that these topics will excite, amongst all classes of her members, serious and prayerful reflection, involving as they do the weighty to the Synod, and which necessarily invite attention in interests of this and future generations. Everything connected with the well-being and efficiency of the Church, whose Protestant doctrines, discipline, and formularies, are the inheritance which ought to be handed down to posterity unimpaired, will depend, under Providence, upon the character which she, as now called upon, may give to herself, as an Institution synodically organized with all the authority of law. Everything will depend upon the nature and provisions of the Constitution which it will be the first duty of the Synod to construct : everything in that Constitution will depend upon the opinions and votes of the members of the Synod ; whilst the views and votes of the lay representatives in it, will depend upon the prevailing opinion of the Church in the constituencies throughout the Diocese, and upon the instructions which they will have received from the electors. Nor can any Constitution, nor any article in a Constitution, nor any thing else, be enacted, without their concurrence. Neither is it to be supposed that the clergy will fail to yield due respect to the well understood and expressed wishes of the great body of the Church. It is, therefore, of the utmost moment that clear and intelligent principles and opinions relative to the several foregoing topics, and to others which may hereafter come under review, should be formed and diffused amongst the Laity generally, in order that, at the elections, they may instruct their delegates, and that, " when the time shall arrive, those delegates may appear in Synod with the weight which must always attach to the opinions of the masses, and be enabled to discharge their important functions with satisfaction to themselves, and benefit to the Church at large."

The Association have now only to renew the expression of their readiness to confer, on all occasions, with their brethren of the Laity, in whatever section of the country they reside ; to invite and welcome them as fellow-members of the Institution ; and to request that their prayers may be blended with their own, for a blessing from Above upon the objects and operations of the Association.

QUEBEC, 24th Novr., 1858.

GEO. HALL,

PRESIDENT.

R. POPE,

SECRETARY.

APPENDIX

A.

PROPOSED CONSTITUTION

FOR THE SYNOD OF THE

DIOCESE OF QUEBEC.

ARTICLE I.

A Synod of the Bishop, Clergy, and Laity, members of the United Church of England and Ireland, in the Diocese of Quebec, shall be held on the third Wednesday in (June), in each year, in the City of Quebec ; but a majority of the Synod may appoint such other place within the Diocese as they may deem advisable for the then next meeting.

ARTICLE II.

The Bishop shall have power to call Special Synods, when he may judge it conducive to the good of the Church ; and shall also do so, when applied to, for that purpose, by the Standing Committee.

ARTICLE III.

The Synod shall consist of, the Bishop of the Diocese ; of the Clergy of the same, being in Priests' orders, institut⸱

ed or licensed to the cure of souls, or being Principals or
Professors in any College, or head-master of the prepara-
tory school in connection with the same, and not being
under ecclesiastical censure ; of Clergymen who have had
a seat in the Synod, but have become superannuated from
age or infirmity ; and of Lay representatives to be elected as hereinafter provided.

ARTICLE IV.

The Lay representatives, being members of the United
Church of England and Ireland, shall be of the full age
of twenty-one years, and shall be elected annually, in each
cure, on Wednesday in Easter Week, or at a meeting
convened for the purpose, after due notice, by the clergyman in charge of such cure, or by ten laymen belonging
to the same ; and all Laymen of twenty-one years of age
or upwards, who shall have declared themselves, in writing, in a book to be provided for such purpose, to be
" Members of the United Church of England and Ireland,
and to belong to no other religious denomination," shall
have the right of voting at such meeting ; and, the Minister in charge of the cure, if present, shall preside at the
election ; and, in his absence, or otherwise, the Curate, or
assistant Minister, or the Chairman elected by a majority
of those present.

ARTICLE V.

The Lay delegates shall consist of not more than three
from each cure ; provided, always, that each congregation within the ecclesiastical parish of Quebec, shall be
considered and held to be, for all the purposes of this Constitution, as a separate cure, and entitled to all the privileges of the same ; a certificate of whose election shall be
signed by the Chairman of the Meeting, and laid before
the Synod before his or their admission to a seat or vote.

ARTICLE VI.

If a vacancy shall occur in the representation of any cure, such cure shall proceed, within as little delay as possible, to a new election, in the manner prescribed by Article IV., to supply such vacancy.

ARTICLE VII.

The Bishop shall preside at all meetings of the Synod, and, in case of absence, or otherwise, or of a vacancy in the Episcopate, the Synod shall elect a President *pro tem.*

ARTICLE VIII.

A quorum of the Synod shall consist of eight Clergymen and eight Laymen ; but a smaller number may adjourn.

ARTICLE IX.

There shall be two Secretaries elected at the annual meeting of the Synod, and they shall retain office till their successors are appointed ; one from the Clergy, the other from the Laity, who shall keep regular minutes of all the proceedings of the Synod ; shall record them in books provided for that purpose ; shall preserve all papers, memorials, and other documents ; shall attest the public acts of the Synod, and shall deliver all records and documents to their successors ; the same to have power to appoint an Assistant Secretary.

ARTICLE X.

There shall be a Treasurer of the Synod, elected in the same manner as the Secretaries, and who shall retain office till his successor shall be appointed ; and who shall receive and disburse all monies collected and paid under its authority ; and there shall be two Auditors to be similarly elected, who shall annually inspect, and report on the condition of the accounts, to a Committee to be appointed for the purpose.

ARTICLE XI.

In all matters brought before the Synod, a majority of votes of the members present shall be decisive ; and, if required by three members, the two orders shall vote separately ; in which case, the concurrence of a majority of each order shall be necessary to constitute a decision; the delegation from each cure, in such case, being entitled to but one vote.

ARTICLE XII.

The Bishop shall have the right to reserve any canon resolution, or proceeding, he may disapprove of, within ten days from its passation by the Synod, upon assigning his reasons therefor, in writing, and handing a copy of the same, signed by himself, to each of the two Secretaries, for the information of the Synod ; in which case, the canon, resolution, or proceeding, shall be returned to the Synod for re-consideration at its next meeting, when a majority of each order shall be necessary for its adoption.

ARTICLE XIII.

It shall be the duty of the Synod, at the first meeting thereof, and at every annual meeting subsequently, to elect, from amongst its own members, a Standing Committee, one half of which to be a quorum, to be composed of three clergymen and three lay representatives, with power to fill up vacancies, who shall retain office till their successors shall be appointed.

ARTICLE XIV.

In case of a vacancy in the See, it shall be the duty of the Standing Committee to give notice of such vacancy to every clergyman and representative within ten days from their knowledge thereof ; and, at the same time, to summon a meeting of the Synod to be held within not less than three months after such vacancy, for the election of a Bishop, giving two months' notice thereof.

ARTICLE XV.

At all elections held by the Synod, the clergy and lay representatives shall vote by orders, by ballot ; and a majority of the votes of each order shall determine the choice.

ARTICLE XVI.

Any cure which may be hereafter established, being desirous of uniting with the Synod of this Diocese, shall apply by letter to the Bishop, or the Standing Committee stating the due organization of the cure, the election of churchwardens, and their means of support of a minister, and their willingness to conform to the Constitution of this Diocese, and the Canons of the Synod thereof ; and at the Synod next succeeding the receipt of such application, the Bishop, or Standing Committee, shall communicate the same to the Synod for its decision thereon. Should the Synod make a favourable decision, the cure shall then be considered as in union, and entitled to all the privileges of the same.

ARTICLE XVII.

In the event of a General Assembly or Synod being hereafter established, it shall be the duty of the Diocesan Synod, at its first meeting thereafter, to elect such number of delegates as shall be deemed necessary to represent the Diocese in such General Assembly or Synod ; provided, always, that one half, at least, of such representatives shall be laymen.

ARTICLE XVIII.

Any proposition for amending or altering this Constitution, must be introduced in writing, and leave obtained for the consideration of the same at the next meeting of the Synod ; and, if then approved by majorities of not less than two-thirds of the Clergy and Lay delegates respectively, it shall be adopted.

APPENDIX

B.

---

19 & 20 VICTORIA, CAP. 121.

An Act to enable the Members of the United Church of England and Ireland in Canada, to meet in Synod.

Whereas doubts exist whether the Members of the United Church of England and Ireland, in this Province, have the power of regulating the affairs of their Church, in matters relating to discipline, and necessary to order and good government, and it is just that such doubts should be removed in order that they may be permitted to exercise the same rights of self-government that are enjoyed by other religious communities ; therefore, Her Majesty, by and with the advice and consent of the Legislative Council and Assembly of Canada, enacts as follows :—

I. The Bishops, Clergy, and Laity, members of the United Church of England and Ireland, in this Province, may meet in their several Dioceses, which are now, or may be hereafter constituted in this Province, and in such manner and by such proceedings as they shall adopt, frame constitutions and make regulations for enforcing discipline in the Church, for the appointment, deposition, deprivation or removal of any person bearing office therein, of whatever order or degree, any rights of the Crown to the contrary notwithstanding, and for the convenient and orderly management of the property, affairs and interests of the Church in matters relating to and affecting only the said

Church, and the officers and members thereof, and not in any manner interfering with the rights, privileges or interests of other religious communities, or of any person or persons not being a member or members of the said United Church of England and Ireland : Provided always, that such constitutions and regulations shall apply only to the Diocese or Dioceses adopting the same.

II. The Bishops, Clergy, and Laity, Members of the United Church of England and Ireland, in this Province, may meet in General Assembly within this Province, by such Representatives as shall be determined and declared by them in their several Dioceses ; and in such General Assembly frame a Constitution and regulations for the general management and good government of the said Church in this Province : Provided always, that nothing in this act contained shall authorise the imposition of any rate or tax upon any person or persons whomsoever, whether belonging to the said Church or not, or the infliction of any punishment, fine, or penalty upon any person, other than his suspension or removal from any office in the said Church, or exclusion from the meetings or proceedings of the Diocesan or General Synods ; and provided also, nothing in the said constitutions or regulations, or any of them, shall be contrary to any law or statute now or hereafter in force in this Province.

An Act to explain and amend the Act intituled " An Act to enable the Members of the United Church of England and Ireland in Canada, to meet in Synod."

Whereas doubts exist whether in the Act passed in the Session held in the nineteenth and twentieth years of Her Majesty's Reign, intituled, " An Act to enable the Members of the United Church of England and Ireland in Canada, to meet in Synod," sufficient provision is made for the Representation of the Laity of the United Church of England and Ireland in the Synods by the said Act authorized to be held, and it is expedient that such doubts should be removed : Therefore, Her Majesty, by and with the advice and consent of the Legislative Council and Assembly of Canada, enacts as follows :—

I. For all the purposes of the aforesaid Act, the Laity shall meet by representation ; and until it shall be otherwise determined by the Synod in each Diocese, one or more delegates (not exceeding three in any case,) may be elected at the annual Easter meetings in each parish, mission, or cure within the Diocese, or in cases where there may be more than one congregation in any parish, mission, or cure, then in each such congregation, or at meetings to be specially called for the purpose by each Clergyman having a separate cure of souls ; and all laymen within such parish mission, or cure, or belonging to such congregation, of the full age of twenty-one years, who shall declare themselves, in writing, at such meetings, to be Members of the United Church of England and Ireland, and to belong to no other Religious Denomination, shall have the right of voting at such election. Each delegate shall receive from the Chairman of the meeting a certificate of his election, which he shall produce, when called upon so to do, at the Synod ; and the first meeting of such Synod shall be called by the Bishop of the Diocese at such time and place as he shall think fit : Provided always, that no business shall be transacted by the Synod of any Diocese unless at least one fourth of the Clergy of such Diocese shall be present, and at least one fourth of the Congregations within the same be represented by at least one delegate.

II. All proceedings heretofore had in any Diocese under the aforesaid Act, which have been conformable to the provisions of this Act, shall be held to be valid, as if the same had taken place after the passing of this Act.